Sweet Tamales for Purim

by
Barbara Bietz

illustrated by
John Kanzler

August House, Inc.
Atlanta

Everyone was invited to the Purim party in our little desert town. Some folks were traveling by horse and buggy, some by train. Even the mayor was coming. So was my best friend, Luis.

"We wear costumes on Purim," I told Luis. "Mama is making me a crown of flowers. I want to be like Queen Esther, the hero of the Purim story. Who would you like to be?"

"I'd like to be a *vaquero*," Luis said. "*Vaqueros* are brave, too! They are expert riders and save cattle from danger."

I drew pictures on my slate board to tell Luis the story of Purim, since his family celebrates different holidays from mine. I told him how Evil Haman plotted to harm the Jews in the city of Shushan.

Queen Esther's uncle, Mordecai, told her about Haman's plot. Esther had not told the king that she was Jewish. She told him now, hoping the king would stop Haman's plot - and he did. The king honored Esther's pleas, and the Jewish people were saved!

"When someone says Haman's name during Purim, there's lots of booing and shouting," I explained. I showed Luis my wooden grogger, a noise-maker especially for Purim.

"Rebecca, can I bring my maracas?" Luis asked.

"Yes!" I clapped my hands. "Maracas are perfect for Purim. Together, we'll make lots of noise!"

Our goat Kitzel is my other best friend. She is going to pull a cart with bells so she can join the fun, too. I tied a gold ribbon around her neck. "Such a pretty girl!" I hugged Kitzel.

Luis patted her head.

"We'll need hamantaschen for the party," I said. "Mama says I'm old enough to make them this year. Come help me, Luis."

"Haman-what?" asked Luis.

"Hamantaschen! Sweet, flakey cookies bursting with poppy seeds or fruit. This year we'll use the apricot jam that mama made. I love how hamantaschen are shaped in triangles, just like Haman's hat."

We measured the flour, sugar, and freshly-churned butter, and then added eggs from our chicken, Henny. We mixed until our arms ached.

Next, we rolled out the dough and cut it into little circles. I showed Luis how to spread the jam and pinch the dough into little triangles. Soon, our hamantaschen were ready to bake.

A sweet scent filled the air.

Mama said our little house smelled like love.

We took our hamantaschen out of the oven so, so carefully.
They were a perfect golden color, like fresh straw.

While the hamantaschen cooled, Luis and I went outside to play marbles under the shade of our fig tree, while Mama hung her best tablecloth to dry.

"Luis!" I called. "Where is Kitzel? She never leaves the yard!"

"Maybe she ran away," Luis said.

"Maybe she got pricked by a cactus," I said. "Or caught in a tumbleweed. Or stuck in the river!"

Luis patted my arm. "We'll find her."

We looked in the barn. Only our horse Goldie, no Kitzel.

We looked in the chicken coop. Only Henny, no Kitzel.

We looked in Mama's vegetable garden. Only little green sprouts, no Kitzel.

Where could she be?

Luis and I felt sad, very sad. One sad queen and one sad *vaquero*.

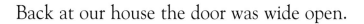

Back at our house the door was wide open.

"Kitzel!" I shouted. I wrapped my arms around her neck.

Luis patted her head.

There were crumbs everywhere.

"Oh, Kitzel! What have you done? You ate all of our hamantaschen!"

Mama walked in after us. "Oy, vey!"

"Can we bake more?" Luis asked.

Mama shook her head. "No more flour or sugar or eggs or butter. No more apricot jam. I'm afraid there will be no hamantaschen this year."

Purim was ruined. I had to fix it. For Mama, for Luis, and for me.

"Luis," I said. "Do you have flour and apricot jam at your house?"

"Let's go see!"

We ran to Luis's house, kicking up dust along the way.

Luis's mama checked their cupboards. "We have some masa flour and some raisins."

"Masa flour?" I asked.

"Flour made from corn," Luis said. "We use it to make tamales."

"Tamales?"

Luis nodded.

"With raisins?"

"Sweet tamales!" Luis smiled a giant *vaquero* smile.

"Sweet tamales for Purim!" we said at the very same time.

First, Luis soaked corn husks in warm water. We measured masa flour, butter, sugar, cinnamon, and water. We mixed until our arms ached. When the husks were soft, Luis showed me how to spread the mixture on the corn husks and fill them with raisins and more sugar and cinnamon. His mama steamed the tamales in a giant pot.

The scent of sweet tamales filled the air.

"*Que bueno!*" said Luis's mama. "*Nuestra casa huele a amor.*"

Luis's house smelled like love, too!

We tied thin ribbons of corn husks around our tamales. We tucked them into baskets and carried them oh-so-carefully to my house.

"Sweet tamales for Purim?" Mama asked, glancing at our baskets.

We held our breath.

"Why not?" Mama asked.

We saved Purim! Luis and I smiled giant, best-friend smiles.

On the day of the party, Kitzel carried our baskets of sweet tamales in her cart.

Author's Note

In the late 1800s, when pioneers settled in the Southwest, life was often lonely and isolated. In towns like Santa Fe and Tucson, communities were formed by people of different backgrounds who came together to build better lives. This story is a work of fiction inspired by a true event. In 1886, the Hebrew Ladies Benevolent Society of Tucson, Arizona planned a Purim Ball for the entire community. At the time, the local newspaper referred to the celebration as "the most brilliant social event in the history of Tucson."

Purim is a Jewish festival that involves the re-telling of the story of Queen Esther and Mordecai and how they saved the Jewish people. Centuries ago, King Ahashuerus ruled the land where many Jews lived. He held a pageant to find a new queen and chose Esther. Queen Esther was Jewish but kept her true identity hidden from the king. Mordecai was a leader of the Jewish people and Esther's older cousin, often referred to as her uncle. When he refused to bow down to Haman, the king's advisor, Haman set a plan in motion to harm all the Jews in the land. Mordecai tells Queen Esther of Haman's evil plot. Esther carefully plans a way to reveal the truth about her identity to the king and foil Haman's plot. King Ahashuerus honors Esther's pleas and the Jews are saved.

With thanks and appreciation to Chris Barash for fostering the creation of so many meaningful stories.
—BLB

For Lorelei.
—JK

Text © 2019 Barbara Bietz
Illustration © 2019 John Kanzler

Published 2019 by August House LittleFolk
August House, Inc
augusthouse.com

Book Design by Graham Anthony

Printed by Pacom Korea

10 9 8 7 6 5 4 3 2 1   PB

ISBN 978-1-947301-61-0

Library of Congress Control Number:2019943613

022030.9K1/B1475/A5